Reycraft Books
55 Fifth Avenue
New York, NY 10003

Reycraftbooks.com

Reycraft Books is a trade imprint and trademark of Newmark Learning, LLC.

This edition is published by arrangement with China Children's Press & Publication Group, China.
© China Children's Press & Publication Group

Educators and Librarians: Our books may be purchased in bulk for promotional, educational,
or business use. Please contact sales@reycraftbooks.com.

This is a work of fiction. Names, characters, places, dialogue, and incidents described either are
the product of the author's imagination or are used fictitiously. Any resemblance to actual
persons, living or dead, is entirely coincidental.

Sale of this book without a front cover or jacket may be unauthorized. If this book is
coverless, it may have been reported to the publisher as "unsold or destroyed" and may have
deprived the author and publisher of payment.

Library of Congress Control Number: 2020908377

ISBN: 978-1-4788-6975-7

Printed in Guangzhou, China.
4401/0620/CA22000850
10 9 8 7 6 5 4 3 2 1

First Edition Hardcover published by Reycraft Books 2020

Reycraft Books and Newmark Learning, LLC, support diversity and the First Amendment,
and celebrate the right to read.

Lemon Butterfly

by Cao Wenxuan  illustrated by Roger Mello

A lemon butterfly searches for a field of flowers.
Its vivid colors and the way it flies are

beautiful.

"I must find a field of flowers!" the butterfly says.

To a butterfly, a field of flowers is the most beautiful thing in the world.

And as it moves, the vision of a flower field flashes before its eyes.

Scintillating!

But the lemon butterfly finds itself in the barren wilds.

Before it, a wide river rumbles.

The lemon butterfly gazes at the vast river.

Frightened.

It flies over the river before turning back to shore.

It takes refuge on a branch. *Trembling.*

The river flows on like a flock of doves
rattling their wings toward the sky.

"I must find a field of flowers!" the lemon butterfly's heart murmurs.

Again, it soars across the big river.

Wind whips over the water, nearly crushing the butterfly against the spray, but it perseveres.

Perhaps there is a field of flowers ahead.

It hears the rumbling of the waves. But the murmuring of its heart is louder.

"I must find that *field of flowers!*"

It finally crosses the river,
but beyond are even more barren wilds.

It keeps flying.

The spring sun shines radiant and golden,
sizzling high in the sky.

A bald mountain stands in its way.
White clouds shroud the peak.

"I must find a field of flowers!"

The lemon butterfly begins to fly *higher* and *higher* and *higher*.

it crosses the big mountain.

One day, as the lemon butterfly flits over a pasture, it catches a whiff of fragrance.

Its tired wings fill with strength.

The scent comes from a horse's hoofprints along a country path.

The lemon butterfly sniffs—an intoxicating smell!

It is certain the horse must have stomped across a field of flowers. The field can't be far.

It begins to follow the trail of hoofprints.

Hoofprints, hoofprints, and more hoofprints...

Fragrance, fragrance, and more fragrance...

But now the scent is getting fainter.

The lemon butterfly hovers, doubtful, over the prints.

It worries as the hoofprints disappear.

When it sees a white horse, it finally realizes it has gone in the wrong direction.

Too tired to fly any longer, it lands on the horse's ear.

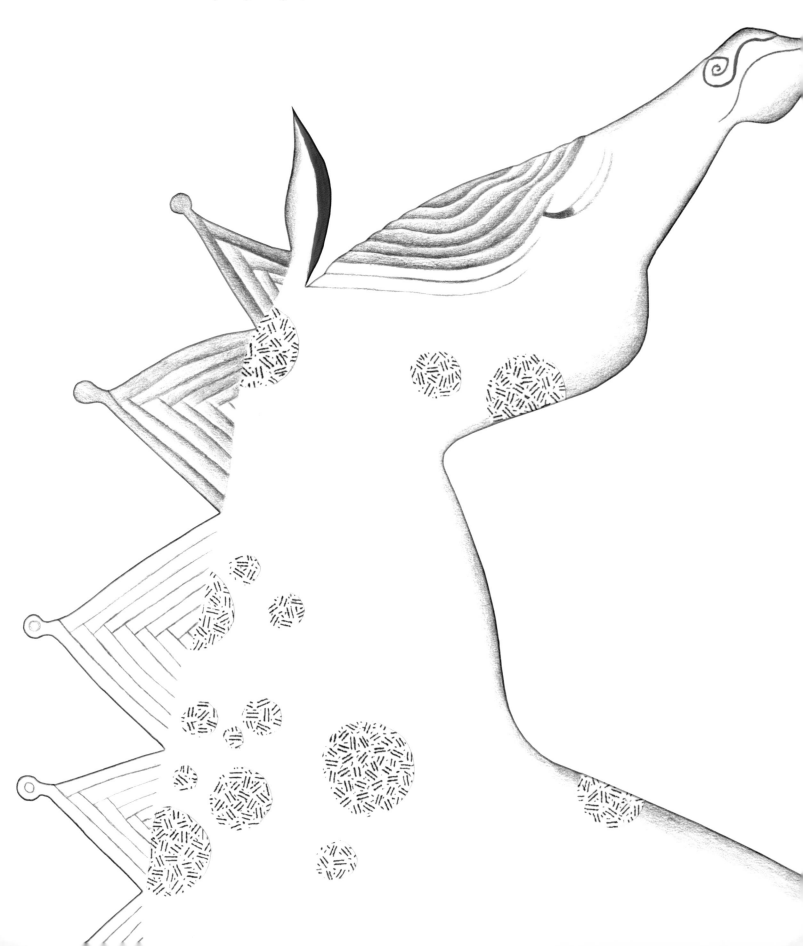

Darkness settles in.

Under the moonlight, the horse whispers,
"It is true, there was indeed a vast field of flowers."

The next day, before sunrise, the lemon butterfly bids the horse farewell and begins to follow the hoofprints back in the other direction. It flies so quickly that the prints rapidly disappear behind it.

The fragrance grows stronger once again.

According to the white horse, the field of flowers lies just beyond the low hills.

The hills appear before the lemon butterfly.

But when it flies over them, what it sees makes it scream.

The field is flooded!

A watery pool.

The air is still. The pool is like a mirror.

The flowers float crystal clear under the water.

The lemon butterfly
hovers close to the surface.
It sniffles as it flies.

Tears drip into the water, forming ripples.
The flowers seem to waver like a brilliant dream.

They bloom under the clear water.
The water magnifies the flowers, making them look especially big.

The lemon butterfly dives toward the water.
It flutters its wings and ascends again.

The underwater flowers are alluring.

Mesmerizing.

The lemon butterfly dives toward the water again and again.

It stops, silently gliding on the surface like a silk ribbon.

After some time, it tries to rise from the water.

But there is nowhere to rest, so it continues to hover.

The flowers seep like tea into the water,
sending their fragrance into the air.

The lemon butterfly dives one last time.
But this time, it doesn't fly up anymore.

It spreads its beautiful wings and quietly
floats on the still water...

...becoming

a lemon butterfly fish.

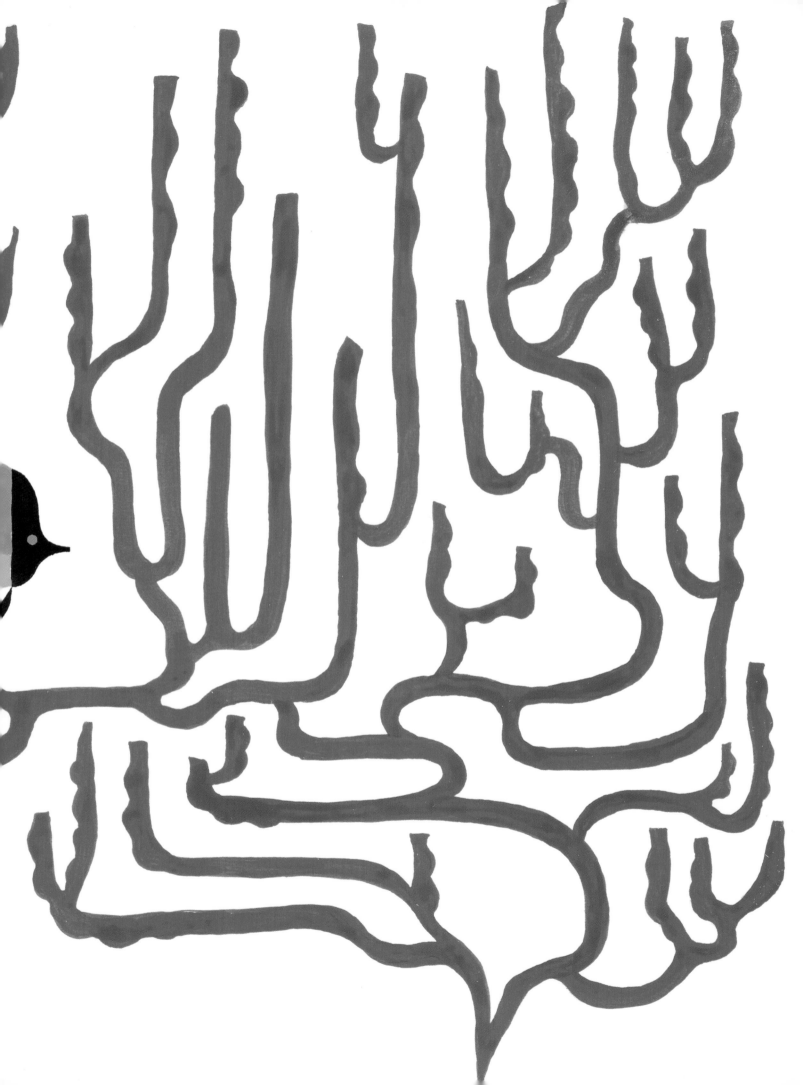

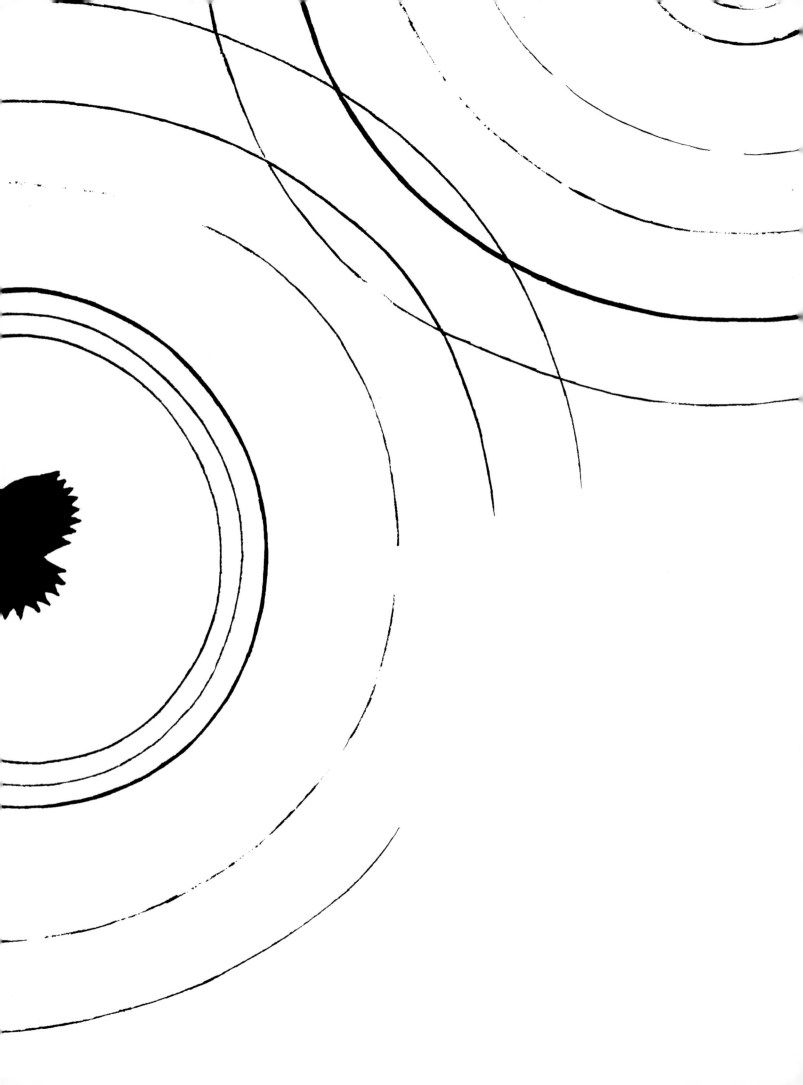